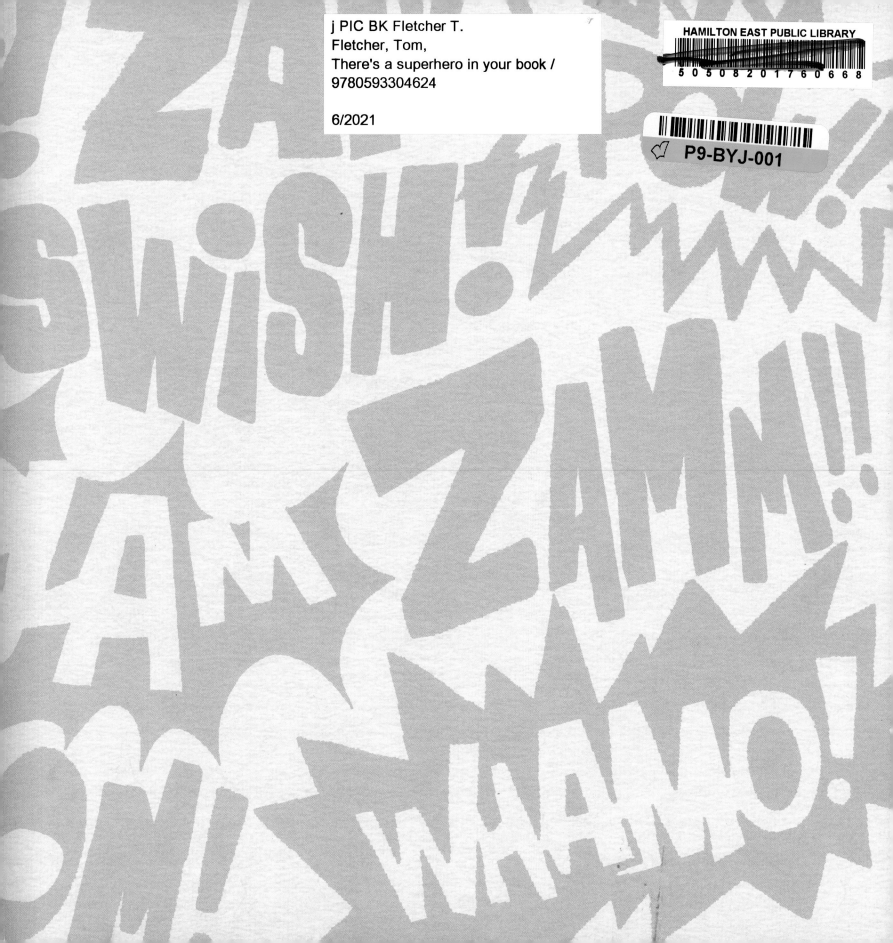

There's a SUPERHERO IN YOUR BOOK

Written by TOM FLETCHER

Illustrated by GREG ABBOTT

Random House 🏠 New York

For Buzz, Buddy, and Max –T.F.

For Roland –G.A.

All rights reserved. Published in the United States by Random House Children's Books,
a division of Penguin Random House LLC, New York. Originally published by Puffin Books, an imprint of
Penguin Random House Children's Books, U.K., a division of Penguin Random House Books, U.K., London, in 2020.

Random House and the colophon are registered trademarks of Penguin Random House LLC.

Visit us on the Web! rhcbooks.com

Educators and librarians, for a variety of teaching tools,
visit us at RHTeachersLibrarians.com

Library of Congress Cataloging-in-Publication Data
Names: Fletcher, Tom, author. | Abbott, Greg, illustrator.
Title: There's a superhero in your book / written by Tom Fletcher ; illustrated by Greg Abbott.
Other titles: There is a superhero in your book
Description: First American edition. | New York : Random House Children's Books, [2021] | "Originally published by Puffin Books, an imprint
of Penguin Random House Children's Books, U.K., a division of Penguin Random House Books, U.K., London, in 2020." |
Audience: Ages 3–7. | Audience: Grades K–1. | Summary: Invites the reader to help Superhero save the book from the Scribbler by lifting it,
concentrating, tapping pages, and more.
Identifiers: LCCN 2020014954 | ISBN 978-0-593-30462-4 (hardcover) |
ISBN 978-0-593-30463-1 (ebook)
Subjects: CYAC: Superheroes—Fiction. | Supervillains—Fiction.
Classification: LCC PZ7.F6358 Thg 2021 | DDC [E]—dc23

MANUFACTURED IN CHINA
10 9 8 7 6 5 4 3 2 1
First American Edition

What was that?

It's a

SUPERHERO!

Wow—there's a superhero in your book!

And he's here to save your book from . . .

THE SCRIBBLER!

Oh no! The Scribbler is scribbling
all over your book with her crayons!

Let's see if Superhero's **SUPERPOWERS** can stop her. How about **super strength**?

Power up Superhero's super strength by **LIFTING** the book high in the air, then turn the page. . . .

Oh dear. The Scribbler has scribbled a big, strong GORILLA in your book!

(I don't think Superhero's super strength is strong enough to take on a big, strong gorilla.)

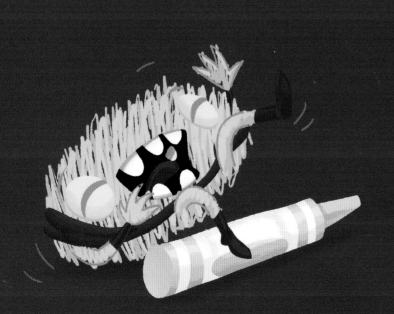

You'd better turn the page quickly. . . .

Let's try something else.
I KNOW! **WATER!**

Concentrate really hard
to help Superhero **WASH** the
Scribbler away.

1, 2, 3 . . .

Look!
The Scribbler scribbled herself
an umbrella just in time.

What will she scribble next?

OH NO—she's scribbled some
NASTY SCRIBBLE BAD GUYS!

We'll have to get rid of them QUICKLY,
or your book will be FULL of SCRIBBLES.

I KNOW!
Maybe Superhero can use *SUPER SPEED!*

TAP all the Scribbles quickly to power up Superhero's super speed.

WOW, great tapping!

But—**UH-OH**—what's happening on the next page?

And now they've captured
all his friends!

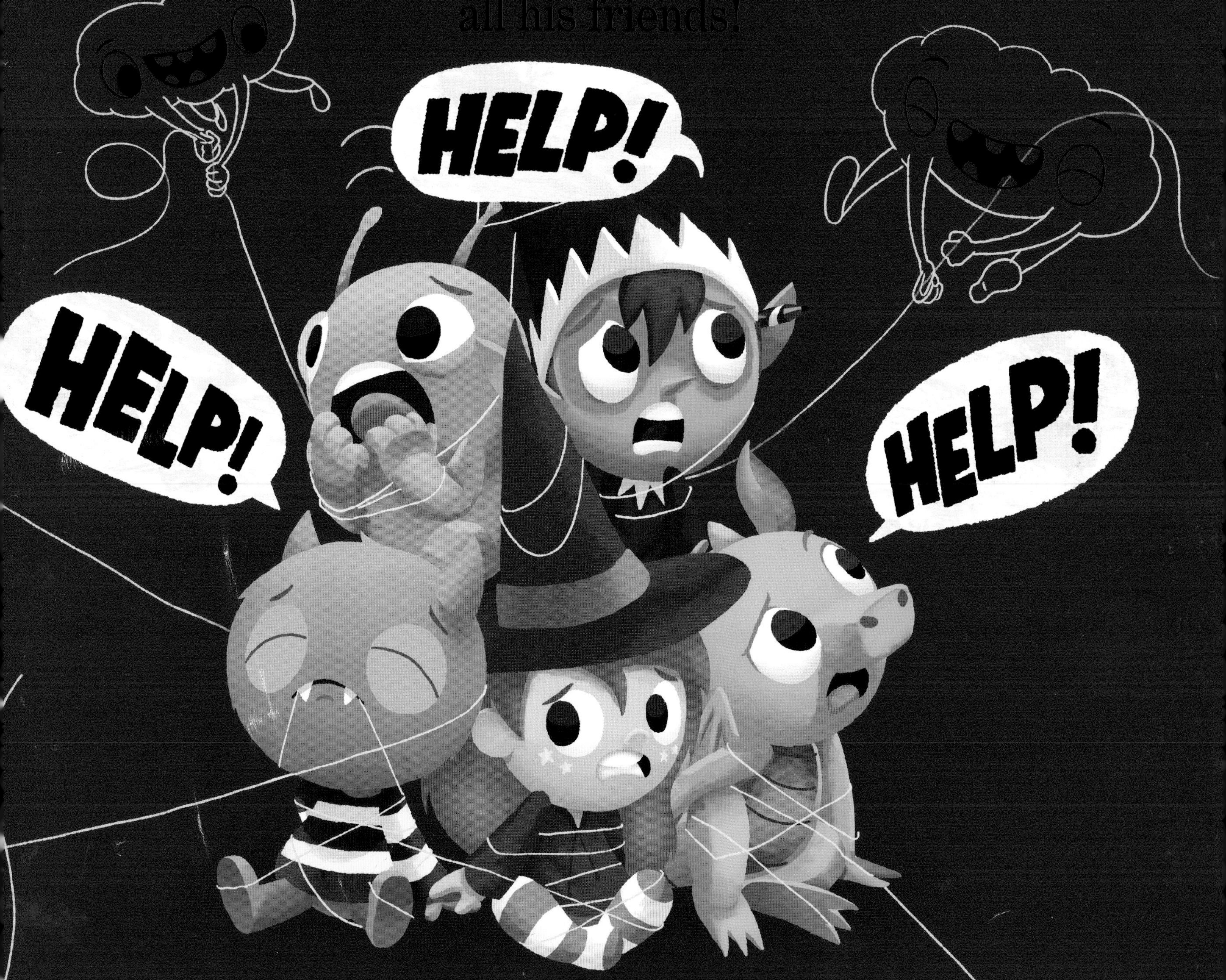

WHAT CAN WE DO?

Maybe Superhero can reach over and untie them
by being **super stretchy**!

STRETCH your arms out
as FAR as you can
to show Superhero how to do it!

Well done! Now turn the page. . . .

OWWW!

Oh dear!
He's all stretched out of shape.
Poor Superhero!

Why don't you blow a **SUPER KISS**
to make him feel better?

Ahhh! That's much better.

Your kindness has made
Superhero feel all super and warm inside.

The strongest superpower of all
ISN'T super strength,
water powers,
super speed,
OR super stretching!

The greatest superpower
is something we *all* have inside . . .

SUPER KINDNESS!

Let's all blow the Scribbler a kiss!

IT WORKED!

Your super kiss and the power of being kind have melted the Scribbler's meanness!

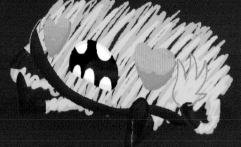

AND all the friends are free!

Good job, Superhero!

Now that the Scribbler isn't mean anymore,
it's time for her to fly away and do some *nice*
scribbling somewhere else—like a coloring book!

WHOOSH the book around in the air
to charge up Superhero's super flying power.

Ready? 1, 2, 3 . . . !

WHOOSH!

Wow, off they go into the world.

I hope Superhero
comes back to help fix
the big hole he's made!

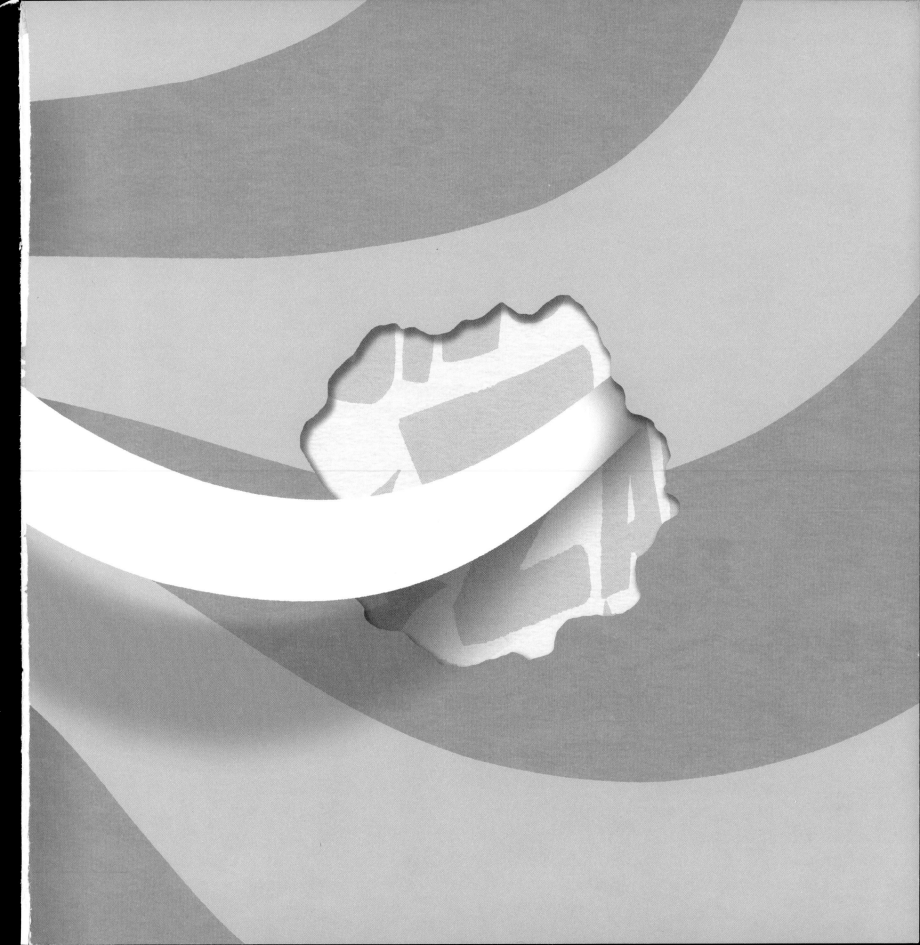